Contents

c 5

Learning Media®

The Escapee

by Johanna Mary

"Jessie, your cousin's here!" called Aunt Maria.

"Hi, Sara," Jessie said, emerging from her room clutching a book – a mystery, judging by the cover. She looked impatient to get back to her book. Jessie was always like that when I visited.

At lunch, Aunt Maria struggled to make conversation while Jessie read. She had a book in one hand and a sandwich in the other. Jessie read all afternoon … and all through dinner. As soon as she'd eaten, she went to her room. I guessed she went in there to read.

Through my bedroom window, I watched the sun set over the ocean. Mom never listened when I told her I didn't like coming here. She thought I enjoyed staying at the beach, and maybe I would if I had someone to hang out with.

As the sun crept below the horizon, I saw him. A tall, skinny man in dark glasses was standing on the boardwalk, staring at the house. Then he began writing in a notebook. He looked up, this time right at me. He seemed startled and hurried away.

"OK, Jessie," Aunt Maria said at breakfast the next morning. "I want you to take Sara to the beach today."

At the beach, Jessie lay on her towel and read. I had a book, too, but I felt restless. I gazed down the beach – and there was the strange man again.

He was sitting on a piece of driftwood writing in the same notebook. He frowned in my direction, but he was wearing sunglasses, so I couldn't tell if he was looking at me.

"Jessie!" I said, touching her shoulder. "That man – do you know him?"

Jessie squinted toward where I was pointing. "He looks kind of familiar, but I'm not sure where I've seen him," she said, turning back to her book.

"I saw him outside your house last night."

I was amazed. Jessie didn't seem very interested. How could she bury her nose in a mystery when a real one might be going on around us?

Aunt Maria made Jessie take me to the market on Saturday, where I saw the man for the third time. He was still wearing those dark glasses. He obviously saw me staring because he quickly turned and tried to slip into the crowd. As he did, something fell from his pocket.

"Jessie, come on!" I yelled.

"Where are you going?" She didn't look happy, but I didn't stop to explain. I raced over to where the man had been standing. On the ground was a key. "I wonder what it's for," I said excitedly. Possibilities whirled through my mind. Did it unlock a safe? – a stolen car? – a secret headquarters?

"It's only a key. Big deal!" said Jessie.

"We've got to find out what it's for," I said. We pushed through the crowd toward the beach where I'd seen the man heading. Out on the boardwalk, I glimpsed him in the distance, then he disappeared.

With Jessie panting after me, I ran. We looked into the yard of every house, finally coming to a blue cottage. There he was, standing in the yard. He was searching his pockets and looked frustrated.

"Excuse me," I called. "Is this yours?" I held up the key.

The man came forward and took it. "I don't appreciate being followed," he said curtly. He returned to the porch and unlocked his front door.

I was disappointed. It was only his house key. At least I had a chance to talk to him, I thought, but I knew I had to be quick before he went inside. "I saw you looking at our house the other day," I said.

"Listen," he replied, turning. "I just want to be left alone."

"Why?" I asked. I didn't know what he was talking about.

"Sara!" said Jessie. She was starting to look really worried. "Let's go."

The man moved toward us and took off his glasses. His eyes were bright and harsh. "Quit following me."

"We're not," I replied, feeling my knees shaking. "You've been following us." I forced my voice to stay steady.

He scrutinized my face. "Don't you know who I am?"

I was bewildered, but Jessie's face flushed. "You're Stan Savage from *Savage Valley*," she gasped. She was the most animated I'd seen her since I'd arrived. "Don't you ever watch that show, Sara?"

"No," I replied. "Why have you been spying on us?" I said turning back to the man.

"Shhh," said Jessie elbowing me before breaking into a huge smile. "It's my favorite show," she enthused.

"Well, I'm sorry I was rude," the man said grudgingly. "I came to this place to get away from people, and I guess I'm a little oversensitive. Why do you think that I was spying on you?"

"The dark glasses, the notebook, and I've seen you staring at me in three different places. Every time I noticed you, you ran away," I replied suspiciously.

The man shook his head. "Well, I guess that must have looked a little strange, but whenever anyone notices me, I think they're going to harass me about the last episode. It's terrible when I'm in the city. I can't walk down the street because people treat me like an evil villain. They forget that I'm an actor."

"Then why do you have that notebook?" I asked, still suspicious.

"I write poetry," he replied. "I'm hoping this place will inspire me. Look, I have to go," he said suddenly. "Maybe I'll see you around."

"Sure," I said.

"Sure!" said Jessie, an excited echo.

Jessie chattered nonstop on the way home. "How amazing. I can't believe Stan Savage is here!" she said. "That show's based on a book. I could lend it to you if you like," she said hesitantly.

"OK," I replied. "I'd like that." I smiled, although I knew she was only being nice because I'd found Stan Savage – but it was a start. Besides, now I was curious about *Savage Valley*. His character must do some pretty bad things for people to get worked up enough to harass him. Maybe this would be another mystery to solve.

illustrations by Donna McKenna

Lost in the Ocean

by Maggie Lilleby

Swallowed by the Ocean?

On December 5, 1945, five Avenger torpedo bombers, code-named Flight 19, took off from Fort Lauderdale, Florida. They never returned, and no trace of the planes or their crews has ever been found. What happened to them remains a mystery – one of the mysteries of the Bermuda Triangle.

What Is the Bermuda Triangle?

You won't find the Bermuda Triangle marked on any maps. However, if you were to draw a line across the Atlantic Ocean from Miami to Bermuda, down to Puerto Rico, and back to Miami, you'd have identified an area with a reputation for mystery and danger.

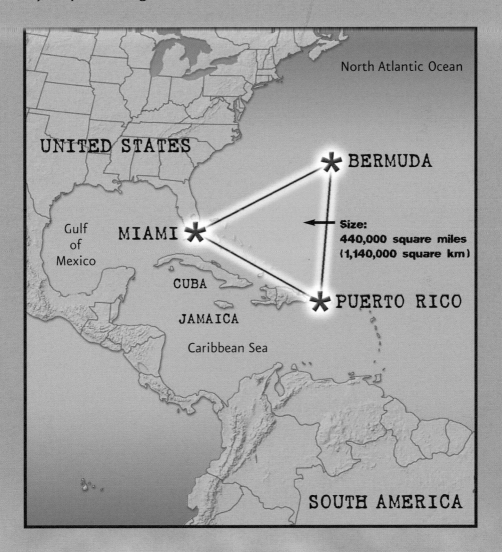

North Atlantic Ocean

UNITED STATES

* BERMUDA

Gulf of Mexico

MIAMI *

← Size: 440,000 square miles (1,140,000 square km)

CUBA

* PUERTO RICO

JAMAICA

Caribbean Sea

SOUTH AMERICA

Strange Happenings

For hundreds of years, sailors told stories of ships going missing in this part of the ocean. Then, in the twentieth century, several planes simply disappeared, leaving no survivors or wreckage. The idea of a mysterious area where ships and planes vanished without a trace caught people's imaginations.

In the 1950s, many newspaper articles and books suggested that the disappearances were due to alien forces. The name Bermuda Triangle was first used in 1964.

Some ships and planes in the area reported unusual events such as a loss of power and communication, spinning compasses, or radio interference. Others reported weird lights in the sky, **whiteout** conditions, unexplained losses or gains in time, or UFO sightings.

whiteout: when fog, cloud, or snow blends with the horizon to make everything seem white

Incidents Timeline

March, 1918
The USS *Cyclops* disappears while sailing between Barbados and Daltimore, Maryland. The ship, its cargo, and 309 people vanish.

December, 1945
Flight 19's five bombers go missing. A search plane sent out to look for the missing planes also disappears.

December, 1948
A plane carrying thirty-one passengers disappears 50 miles (88 kilometers) from Miami.

February, 1963
The tanker SS *Marine Sulfur Queen* disappears after radioing in its position in the Florida Straits.

January, 1949
A plane carrying thirteen passengers vanishes between Bermuda and Jamaica after sending out a message that it's on schedule.

13

Mystery versus Science

While many people believe that there is something sinister about this triangle of ocean, scientists believe that the disappearances can be explained. These are some of their views.

• There were often bad weather conditions at the time of the disappearances.

• The planes or ships could have experienced mechanical failure.

• Parts of the Atlantic Ocean are very deep, making it impossible to find wreckage.

• Human error could lead to many accidents, such as a plane crashing due to running out of fuel or a ship hitting a sandbank.

• Many ships and planes cross this area of the ocean successfully.

• The Bermuda Triangle is one of only two places in the world where the needle of a compass points toward true north. Usually it points toward magnetic north. This would explain the unusual behavior of a ship's compass. The other place is in the Pacific Ocean near Japan, and that's also known for strange events.

Compass Variation

The difference between true north and magnetic north is known as compass variation. There can be as much as 20 degrees difference between these two points. If this variation isn't taken into account, a navigator and crew could find themselves hundreds of miles off-course.

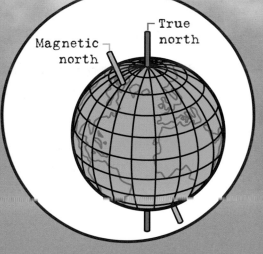

Explorer Christopher Columbus passed through the Bermuda Triangle in 1492. He noted that his ship's compass was behaving strangely and that the ocean seemed to be glowing. He also reported a fireball that circled his ship, a giant waterspout, and a strange whirlwind.

People who believe in the mystery of the Bermuda Triangle have their own explanations. These include:

- The people who vanished from the ships and planes were abducted by aliens.
- There is a "hole in the sky" that sucks people up.
- The Bermuda Triangle is the site of the lost city of Atlantis.
- The forces at work are unknown to science and so cannot be explained.

The story of Atlantis was first told by Plato, a Greek philosopher, around 320 B.C. According to Plato, Atlantis was a beautiful place, with mountains, forests, temples, gardens, and canals that sank beneath the ocean. The legend of Atlantis has fascinated people for thousands of years, but no evidence that Atlantis actually existed has ever been found.

Over the past one hundred years, it's been estimated that more than fifty ships, twenty planes, and one thousand people have disappeared in the Bermuda Triangle. To some people, this is an unusually high number, especially as there is often no reason for the disappearances. Other people say that this stretch of ocean is no more dangerous than any other in the world.

The Mystery Remains

In 1991, the wreckage of five Avenger planes was found off the coast of Florida. At first, it was thought that these were the missing planes of Flight 19. However, close examination showed that they were different. The mystery of Flight 19, along with those of many other ships and planes, remains unsolved.

Fourteen Airmen Still Missing

It's a Mystery

Young people these days are a mystery to me.
Now I know I'm getting no younger.
But I thought I was up with the times.
It seems that's not true any longer.

Why do you wear your caps back to front?
What on earth are these "special fx?"
How many mouthfuls in a megabyte?
How do you read a message in text?

Now, I can still foxtrot,
but techno and hip-hop
are beyond my comprehension.
I can't understand rap
or "whatup" or "phat,"
the language of teenage invention.

What do you do when you're "just hanging out"?
Why talk so loud on the subway?
Why do you crowd in the mall after school
and text friends you've just talked to all day?

But the most mysterious thing of all,
the thing I just can't figure out,
is why do you wear baggy, over-sized pants
and not hold them up with a belt?!

by Ali Everts

illustration by Courtney Hopkinson

LOST and FOUND

by Susan Paris

Characters

Ms. Stanley 1 and Ms. Stanley 2
(identical twins played by the same person)

Wendy

Carlos

J.D.

Scene: *The office of the Lost and Found Department in Eastridge Mall.* **J.D.** *and* **WENDY** *are reading magazines at their desks.* **CARLOS** *is looking for something. The phone rings.*

J.D. *(answering the phone)*: Good morning. Eastridge Mall Lost and Found Department, how can I help you? *(He listens for several moments.)* I'm sorry, I'll have to put you through to our animal control department. One moment, please. *(He puts the phone down.)*

WENDY: We don't have an animal control department.

J.D.: A woman lost her poodle in the parking lot. Officially, that's not part of the mall, so it's not our problem.

CARLOS *(frustrated)*: Has anyone seen my stapler?

MS. STANLEY 1 *(entering)*: My name's Ms. Stanley, and I'd like to report a missing person.

CARLOS: Well, you've come to the right place. Can you tell us what happened?

MS. STANLEY 1: I was shopping with my sister. We were buying our nephew a baseball ... and when I looked up, she'd disappeared.

WENDY: Maybe she's a magician.

MS. STANLEY 1 *(surprised)*: Not that I know of.

CARLOS *(glaring at Wendy)*: Leave this to me, Wendy. Then what happened, Ms. Stanley?

MS. STANLEY 1: I've looked everywhere. I've been searching for the last hour, but I just can't find her.

CARLOS: How would you describe your sister?

MS. STANLEY 1: She's my height, and she has brown curly hair. She was wearing a jacket like mine. We often wear similar clothes. Actually, we're ...

J.D. *(interrupting)*: That should be enough for us to go on. The best thing you can do is go back out there and look for her. We're losing precious time.

MS. STANLEY 1: You're right. I'll go back to the sporting goods store and look some more.

WENDY: Good luck.

    MS. STANLEY 1 *leaves.*

J.D.: Hey, would anyone like some coffee?

WENDY *(glumly)*: We've lost the coffee pot.

CARLOS: I have some tea.

    They're interrupted by **MS. STANLEY 2** *entering.*

WENDY: Still no luck, Ms. Stanley?

MS. STANLEY 2 *(surprised)*: How did you know my –

WENDY *(importantly)*: We're professionals. We're trained to recognize these things. For example, I notice you weren't wearing that scarf earlier.

MS. STANLEY 2 (*confused*): Actually, I was. I put it on this morning.

WENDY: That's strange. I didn't notice it. It must have been hidden by your jacket.

CARLOS (*impatient*): Getting back to the problem at hand, have you looked in all the stores on the first floor, Ms. Stanley?

MS. STANLEY 2: Yes – and the second floor, too.

J.D.: That was quick. Did you check thoroughly?

MS. STANLEY 2 (*hesitant*): Well …

WENDY: She is your sister, you know.

MS. STANLEY 2: You're right. I'll go and take another look.

    MS. STANLEY 2 *leaves.*

J.D. (*shaking his head*): You'd think she'd try harder. She's only been gone a few minutes.

CARLOS: Yes, it does seem a little odd.

They all settle back to what they'd been doing earlier.

MS. STANLEY 1 *(entering and looking flustered)*: This is terrible. Where can she be?

CARLOS *(politely)*: I'm sorry, but I don't think you're being very thorough.

MS. STANLEY 1 *(angrily)*: I think I can be trusted to look for my own sister properly, young man.

CARLOS: But you just ...

MS. STANLEY 1 *(interrupting him)*: Never mind. You're the experts. If you think I need to check again, I'll search the second floor.

MS. STANLEY 1 *leaves.*

WENDY: What a hectic morning. I need a break. Where's the crossword book?

J.D. *(reaching for a newspaper)*: Yes, some peace and quiet would be good. I have some paperwork to catch up on.

MS. STANLEY 2 *(entering)*: Well, no luck. I'm exhausted. I've decided it would be best to wait at the car.

J.D.: Good idea. We were about to suggest that.

MS. STANLEY 2: Well, thank you for your help.

WENDY: No problem.

MS. STANLEY 2 *leaves.*

J.D.: Well, I'm glad that's over. What a difficult customer – why was she so reluctant to follow our advice? Hey, it's almost lunchtime. Who wants a sandwich?

CARLOS: I do.

The phone rings.

J.D.: Oh, come on!

WENDY: I'll get it. *(She picks up the phone.)* Good morning. Eastridge Mall Lost and Found, how can I help you? Yes ... yes, I see. Well, thanks for keeping us informed. *(She hangs up.)* That was Ms. Stanley. She wanted us to know she's on her way to the parking lot. She's certain her sister will be waiting in the car.

CARLOS: She must think we have short-term memory problems.

J.D. *(shaking his head sadly)*: Nobody trusts a professional these days.

illustrations by Scott Pearson

The Mysteries of Migration

by Nic Bishop

GREAT MIGRANTS

Birds are great migrants. Every fall, enormous flocks fly to warmer places where there's plenty of food. Some species travel thousands of miles. Snow geese from northern Canada fly to the United States. Swallows from England fly to South Africa. How do birds find their way across such huge distances? This is a mystery that scientists have only just begun to solve.

One of the most amazing migrants is the bar-tailed godwit, which spends the northern summer in Alaska. In the fall, when they sense the days becoming shorter, the godwits gather in large flocks. Then one day, they begin flying south over the Pacific Ocean to New Zealand. The godwits fly nonstop – if they land in the ocean, they'll drown. The distance is more than 6,500 miles (10,500 kilometers), and it takes four to five days of flying, day and night!

New Zealand is south of the Equator, which means that it's summer there when it's winter in Alaska. The godwits fly to New Zealand because it's warm there and there's plenty to eat. When the southern summer ends, they return for the northern summer in Alaska.

These godwits are preparing to fly north to Alaska at the end of the southern summer.

Stocking Up on Fuel

Before migrating, birds eat huge amounts. The food is digested, and the energy is stored as fat. This gives the birds enough fuel to last them on their incredible journey. When a godwit begins its migratory flight, more than half of its body weight is fat.

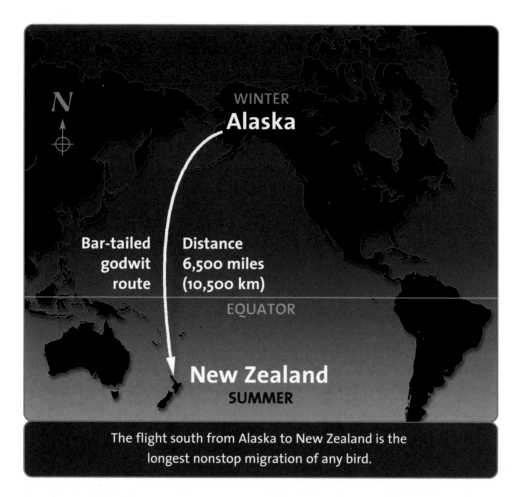

FINDING THEIR WAY

Many migrating birds return to the same small pond or beach year after year. Young ducks, geese, swans, and cranes migrate with adult birds. They learn which way to go from the adults and use rivers, lakes, and mountains that they pass along the way as signposts to guide them the next time they migrate.

The young of most other migrating birds, such as godwits, don't travel with the adults, yet they still seem to know which way to go. How do they find their way to a place they've never been to before?

It appears that these birds are guided by natural instinct. Scientists have discovered that birds have an internal compass that tells them which way is north, south, east, or west. Experiments have shown that birds tell this from the position of the sun as it moves across the sky. At night, they use the movement of the stars to guide them.

However, scientists also noticed that migrating birds still flew the right way on cloudy days and nights when they couldn't see the sun or the stars. They did an experiment to figure out if these birds used more than one way to decide on direction. Tiny hats with magnets inside them were attached to some birds. The scientists discovered that the direction the birds flew depended on the way the magnet was pointing. This indicated that in addition to using the sun and the stars, birds use Earth's magnetic field to guide them.

Earth Is a Magnet

Earth is surrounded by a magnetic field. This field is strongest at the north and south poles. The angle of the field points into Earth at the North Pole and out at the South Pole. Scientists believe that birds can sense both the strength and angle of Earth's magnetic field. They may use this ability to determine direction as well as how far north or south they are.

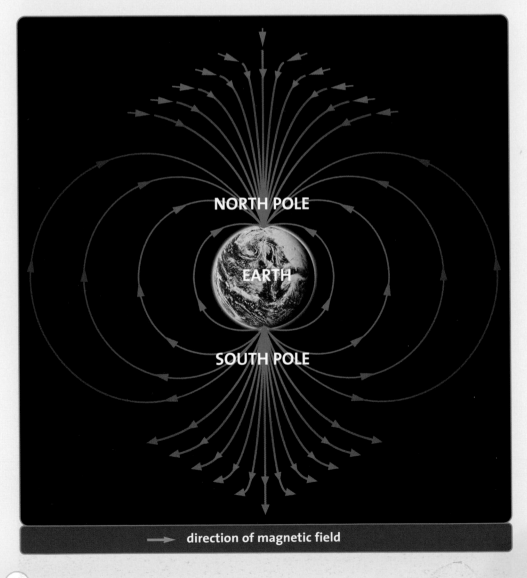

NORTH POLE

EARTH

SOUTH POLE

→ direction of magnetic field

The more scientists study bird migration, the more complicated and amazing it seems. Besides their memory and magnetic fields, there might be other tricks that birds use that we still don't know about. Birds can detect small changes in air pressure, which people can't. They're sensitive to high- and low-pitched sounds as well as to particular smells. The true mystery of migration might be much greater than we can imagine.

Find Out More

If you enjoyed this book, you can read more about **mystery** in these Orbit resources.

Chapter Books

JEAN BENNETT
Illustrated by Gus Hunter

Collections